Egan Mew

A London Comedy, and Other Vanities

Egan Mew

A London Comedy, and Other Vanities

ISBN/EAN: 9783744787291

Printed in Europe, USA, Canada, Australia, Japan

Cover: Foto ©Andreas Hilbeck / pixelio.de

More available books at **www.hansebooks.com**

A LONDON COMEDY

AND

OTHER VANITIES

BY

EGAN MEW

WITH SEVEN REPRODUCTIONS OF PICTURES

BY

MAURICE GREIFFENHAGEN

LONDON

GEORGE REDWAY

1897

LONDON :

PRINTED BY WILLIAM CLOWES AND SONS, LIMITED,

STAMFORD STREET AND CHARING CROSS.

IF THERE CHANCE TO BE ANYTHING
WORTHY IN THIS SLIM VOLUME, IT IS
DEDICATED WITH ADMIRATION AND
WARM AFFECTION TO THE COMRADE OF
MY YOUTH, MY TRIED AND CONSTANT
LIFE-LONG FRIEND, JOHN ROBERT
MANNERS, OF THE MIDDLE TEMPLE.

Some of these verses have appeared in " Temple Bar," the " Graphic," the " Queen," and the " Pall Mall Budget." I am greatly indebted to the editors and proprietors of these journals for permission to reproduce them here, and especially to the " Pall Mall Budget " for the same kindness in regard to four of Mr. Greiffenhagen's illustrations. These, however, have been to some extent redrawn for the purposes of this book.

CONTENTS

LIST OF ILLUSTRATIONS

" Why should one's neighbours fain a care
About our hearts? The only wear
'S a modish mask   "

TO MY FIRST READER

THE candles cast a topaz light
About your room; the fire's bright
On silk and silver. You are dight
>In *robe-de-Thé*.

When, lo! the post is just brought in,
And there, two little notes between,
Lies a small book, in format lean,
>And white array.

I note a touch of welcome fire
Brighten dear eyes, and then expire:
Would I could send "celestial choir"
>To cheer and please you.

You will not care for all that's set,
You hate the note of "mad regret,"
You don't care much for *amourette*—
>Such trifles tease you.

11

But here, but there, across my page,
A phrase may hint that golden age
When I was young and you were sage,
                    When life ran gayer.
Yet life was sad as well, for we
Were haunted by the minstrelsy
That, following Love with mystery,
                    Hints a betrayer.

Though oft we met with straining hearts,
We ne'er forgot those worldly arts
Which made us actors—playing parts—
                    And left us masking.

     *   *   *

I've tangled warp with tangled weft,
The right with wrong, and all that's left
Of a just meaning stands bereft.
                    Yet still I'm asking—

How rang that old true song in air
We used to hear? Despair! Despair!
The voices call—they echo where
                    Once laughter lilted.

     *   *   *

We've left undone those things we ought
(As every Worldly-wiseman taught)
To make our own peculiar thought.
                    We've sometimes jilted

Those who were kind. We've laughed to scorn
Our loved ones, and our vows forsworn.
Dearest of all—cold Death hath shorn
                    Of human fashion.
Hopes that were virgin lie profaned:
We sought for joy, for fortune strained,
The happy gods our prayers disdained,
                    And now the passion

Of our queer world is upside-down,
The cynic's kiss, the lover's frown,
The poet's fame and rogue's renown
                    Grow complicated.
The sour is somewhat sweetly drawn,
In Christian haunts go nymph and faun,
The primal colours of our dawn
                    Fly—dissipated.

But as we say, ' The time goes by,'
And no one cares that I am—I.
And then, of course, the ' psychic cry '
      Is rather silly.
Why should one's neighbours fain a care
About our hearts ? The only wear
'S a modish mask 'gainst cutting air
      And critics chilly.

A few may turn my verse about
And push the ragged edges out :
The wise will sneer ; I have no doubt
      About *their* greeting.
And you were hard to please, I know,
And yet I always long to show
The broken dreams that come, that go,
      To you, my sweeting.

A LONDON COMEDY

Prologue

THE SPIRIT OF MODERN COMEDY

L'esprit Moqueur ! the only gnome
Whose presence now is always sure :
In London town he's free to roam—
    L'esprit Moqueur.

He'll win you with a laughing lure,
Deep in your heart he'll make his home—
All other loves you'll then abjure.

He'll haunt your house from base to dome,
And sap your soul, this gay *flâneur*,
Make Death a jest as light as foam—
    L'esprit Moqueur.

15

Dramatis Personæ

"She". . . Diane Carruthers.
"He". . . . Vernon Aylmer.
"Another" . . The Hon. John Adair.

I

*A dinner-party. "She" is talking in a lively way with
"Another." "He" is not included in the conversation.*

When first we met, a year ago,
I thought you rather *too* coquette;
You guessed I should prove *borné*—slow,
     When first we met.

I'd often watched you, through lorgnette,
I'd often seen you in the Row—
And planned an *entrée* to your set.

You seemed that night all *allegro*,
Handsome and bright and sweet—and yet,
Somehow, you made me feel *de trop*,
     When *first* we met.

"What heaps of things we've learned to know
Since first I fell within your net
   A year ago."

II

*" He " and " She " are on a balcony overlooking the Park
at night.*

A year ago ! no more, my pet.
What heaps of things we've learned to know
Since first I fell within your net
      A year ago.

You've laughed at suitors high and low :
I've noted how (without regret)
You've sacrificed no end of beaux.

I wonder—is your heart to let :
I dream I've gained a chance *morceau*—
Since that dear night you made me fret,
      A year ago.

III

A corner in an old garden. Beehives, a statue of Pan;
hayfields beyond.

We snatched a day from out our lives,
And spent it 'mid the fields of hay:
From London town, from social gyves,
   We snatched a day.

We heard the lark's fresh roundelay,
We watched the bees about their hives,
We joined the summer winds at play.

How is't rusticity contrives
To give blue eyes a tenderer grey?
I thank old Pan (who still survives)
   We snatched that day.

IV

In a conservatory.

No one shall know what came by chance
When we were seated *dos-à-dos*,
And you threw back a tempting glance—
       No one shall know.

Through all the years that come and go
That moment will the rest enhance,
Casting across my world a glow.

Can you recall our next sweet dance?
Could you repeat that action?—so!
Ah! pray forgive, nor look askance,—
       No one shall know !

V

At Henley.

If life be vain, as wise men say,
And we're foredoomed our meed of pain,
Let's laugh throughout our little day—
         If life be vain.

To-morrow I shall catch the train
Which takes *your* party Henley way,
And so we'll meet just once again.

We'll watch together the essay
Of those who mean the sculls to gain ;
An you are by, *living* is play—
         If *life* be vain.

"I have no roses now to fling
Beneath your feet;   "

VI

An "At Home."

To thee, dear Di, I fain would bring
Fortune, and Fame, and Revelry :
These are not mine, I can but sing
            To thee, dear Di.

Others there be who woo and sigh—
The Wit, the Fool, the Hireling :
They bring their wares your heart to buy.

I have no roses now to fling
Beneath your feet; my star's awry—
I send a song on halting wing
            To thee, dear Di.

VII

At Cowes.

On East Cowes Creek I'd love to stay
And in some eyes my fortune seek,
And watch their sparkling, subtle play,
    On East Cowes Creek.

There we may dream that wrong is weak,
And cease to laugh the world away,
Nor hold all life a weary freak.

And yet, the Fates curtail our stay
To just the sweet regatta week.
Adieu! to eyes too kind to slay
    On East Cowes Creek.

"   on the whole,
We'd better laugh, and loose the chain
Of roses.'   "

VIII

A Watteau party in a wood.

We've played our *rôles* of nymph and swain,
And found our masque exceeding droll;
From Season's zenith to its wane
          We've played our *rôles*.

And now you say that "on the whole,
We'd better laugh, and loose the chain
Of roses, ere we reach the goal."

So you, dear Di, will cease to reign
O'er my poor "analytic soul."
How cold 'twill grow; yet there's the gain,
          We've *played* our *rôles*.

IX

In the Park : " She " and " Another " riding. " She "
turning away. " He," also on horseback, in foreground,
looking back.

You turned aside as I went by ;
I longed to speak. You know I tried
To meet the swift light of your eye.
                You turned aside.

Thanks to the philosophic guide
Who talks with you so earnestly,
Who's always with you in the Ride.

Ah ! did you mean my mood to try ?
Hardly, I think ; you could not hide
That you still blush responsively—
                You turned and sighed.

X

St. Peter's, Eaton Square.

We've laughed away the wise men's saws,
And mocked the Fates for many a day.
An earnest mood—a tell-tale pause—
        We've laughed away.

Only the truth was *hasardée*;
Our smiles were based on tears, as cause;
Our songs were doubtful melody.

All life's perfection, all its flaws,
All hasty progress, dull delay,
Religion, love, emotion, laws,
        We've laughed away.

XI

Later.

So you have wed old Jack Adair!
In ropes of pearls you're captive led;
You "felt inclined his lands to share,"
                    So you are wed.

You write me that "old hopes are fled";
You say you know I "shall not care"—
We'll think the past lies cold and dead.

A pretty house in smart Mayfair,
A Berkshire park where oak trees spread,
Outweigh our castles of the air . . .
                    So you are wed.

" One gift the kind gods hold in store :
To dine."

XII

After a Season or two.

A house at which to dine, no more,
You think I think your dwelling fine,
A house where it's not *quite* a bore
        To dine.

We've laughed away all thoughts divine,
We've learnt our jot of worldly lore,
And bowed our last at any shrine.

Yet there's a rite man can't ignore—
Women and song go by, and wine—
One gift the kind gods hold in store:
        To dine.

Envoi.

Looking backward, who shall tell
All the glories—all the lack—
There is Heaven, there is Hell,
　　　　　Looking back.

There lie hopes, a sorry pack,
Rising hopes which quickly fell—
Swift to teach a cynic knack.

Behind—the chimes ring like a knell,
Joy-bells jangle all a-crack;
Happier an we mar no spell—
　　　　　Looking back.

LAGGARD FAME

AFTER much toil and passion
  A poet learned to wear
A smile for life's poor fashion,
  A mask for biting care.

He, faithful to his art, sings,
  Mocking his sense of wrong,
Pain's finger on his heart-strings—
  Sweet music in his song.

Now Fortune seeks a meeting,
  She calls his name one morrow ;
She gets strange tears for greeting ;
  He'd laughed too long with sorrow.

TO TWO FRIENDS

IN MEMORY OF

HUBERT MONTAGUE CRACKANTHORPE.

I

OLD friends! old friends, the name
Rings doubly good
Now, as we count the loss
Of his fair manlihood,
Now, as we cry in bitterness and blame,
Behold! his life is gone—
Lost with the flotsam and the dross—
Inconsequently caught in the ever-lengthening, wan
Trooping of Death, who hunts in merry and un-
    tiring mood
The loved, the beautiful, the brave.
O! could not then the grave—
The horrible, insatiate—
Be this time propitiate
With lesser souls than his, whose soul had grown
Melodiously in concord with our own.

II.

Unto my friends who doubted, wept, despaired,
Disputed, argued, while there yet remained
Uncertainties, and hope with time was gained—
Unto my friends : "If he be gone, if he, indeed,
    has fared
Beyond these bounds of complex destiny,
O, remember and be cheered—
Those who were dear on earth are more endeared,
The thing that pained no longer pains.
Down the cold corridors, within the silent alcoves
    of the dead,
The great renunciations are as storèd gains,
The once poor negatives of life shine newly, bright
As jewels indiademed. Obliterate the dread
Compressed within that day of troubles, that horrific
    night."

III

Comrade of days—the years were yet to be—
Dearest you were to my sweet friends,
Through them to me ;
And now, alas, so soon our converse ends.

'Neath the umbrageous shadow of their tree
Of love, we've met, welcome in fellowship, free
Of amicable highways, cities, and fair meads;
Free of fair speech and courteous, kindly deeds.

IV

Friend, this poor thing is true—
Your voice, remembered, rings,
Still rings the melody anew,
For ever in the hearts whose tenderest note
Has echoed your clear music. In our hearts
Is bound the cherished vision of your face, serene,
    remote,
Crowned with those garlands sad-sweet memory
    brings,
Limned by the deftest, subtlest of the arts,—
The nameless art that neither paints nor sings.

V

Yours were high gifts, and you were ardent, young.
How much achieved! how much is left undone!
Fair and fresh-hued, the cameo of your face
Shone oft with satire, oft with wit,
And oft with merriment was lit,

And oft with genial grace.
The sensitive soft mouth, the clear, firm jaw,
The potent brow, both generous and bold,
The frank grey-blue of eyes without a flaw,
Told of wide views, capacity, and power,
Potentialities the future should unfold—
Blotted from life in one misgotten hour.

VI

Athwart the happiness of golden autumn days,
Athwart the life that seemed of hope compact,
Grew, from no whither, a miasmic haze. .

.   .   .   .

VII

No more the kind heart feels the anguish and the
    gust
Of passion. No more the pain of broken hope or
    trust :
No more the fret and clash of indeterminate
Souls, whose loves, like hates, exterminate.
Never again his nature (sensitive o'er much
But nobly reticent) shall bear the touch

D

Of hands still unattuned to lyric things.
His thoughts suggested, half expressed, on earth,
    shall fly
In beauty and rich lights on high :
No longer clad in modish drapery
To hide ethereal, silver-shining wings.

VIII

Adieu, O Prince of golden hearts.   Adieu,
O rare and happy spirit that we knew.
Ours is the sorrow, ours the empty pain,
Yours is for heritage some wide domain,
Some wider world than ours
Where love, the rose divine,
And friendship, the soul's eglantine,
Afar, in starry bowers,
Develop and outshine
Life's galaxy of flowers.

Christmas, 1896–7.

T'WARDS ARCADIE

A DUOLOGUE

To the Audience.

Our play is short, requiring little casting ;
Two people in a sweet conservatory ;
  Later maybe
  We'll chance to see
This couple trip it into Arcadie,
 Thinking their ecstasy
  For ever lasting.

She. "Our waltz at last! yet let it go,—
 I've danced through one with Hugh Defoe,
 And learned to weigh that guardsman's toe;
  His step is all too dashing."

He. "Yes? Then rest we will and hear the flow
　　Of fiddle and of piccolo;
　　I'll watch . . . . ."

She. 　　　　　　"The dancers?"

He. 　　　　　　　　　　"Ah, no,
　　Your eyelids flashing."

She. "*Monsieur, de grâce* . . . . 'In Arcadie,'
　　I see this waltz is said to be:
　　How sweet the music's melody
　　　　　And fountain plashing."

He. "'In Arcadie'? Have you been there?"

She. "Is it the region of the stair,
　　Far up above the candle's flare,
　　And cymbals clashing?"

He. "Sometimes, perhaps . . . ."

She. 　　　　　"You know it then:
　　You've entered there? Oh, tell me when?

Or is't a land of smoke—and men,
Of *sabretasche* and sashing?"

He. "I've only glanced in once—or twice,—
Just now in handing you an ice,
Something I saw that would entice
All Arcadie."

She. "Indeed! what . . . . lenses did you use?"

He. "Your eyes: their blueness my excuse."

She. "Yours is, I think, too worn a *ruse*
For Arcadie.

But tell me of this happy land—
Do nymphs and swains go hand-in-hand
To airs—like the Hungarian band
Is playing?"

He. "Daphnis and Chloë still are there;—
He binds bright myrtle in her hair.
No whisper comes of carking care,
Of cold heart's slaying . . ."

She. " Go on, I pray."

He.   " There roses bloom ;
     The golden days can know no gloom ;
     Eternal happiness their doom,—
                    So Chloë's saying.

     Yet no one is bored ; bright eyes meet eyes
     Still brighter, for they lack disguise.
     Life sweetly comes, but never flies
                    In Arcadie."

She. " Would I could visit, at season's end,
     The world you paint with cunning blend
     Of colour words, as though you'd send
                    Us all to Arcadie.
     Which is the way ? I'll journey there
     Alone ; the land seems passing fair. . . ."

He. " Not so—*alone ;* they go a-pair
                    In Arcadie."

She. " Oh ! . . . ."

He.   " There's one sweet way, may I
                show how ? "

She. " But—where and when ? "

He.   " Ah ! here and now.
        Dearest, you know, you must allow—
        My heart is breaking."

She. " Sir, you forget ; our waltz is done.
        Through the camellias dancers come . . .
        Your heart, my heart—I think they're one.
                  Is't worth the taking ? "

He. " While there be life, *one* it shall be—
        Yours : yours and mine—no room for three
        In all the breadth of Arcadie."

Envoi

And so, messieurs, we've chanced to see
Two more trip up to Arcadie.
Ah me !
They think the land will ever be
Their property.

IN A SUBURBAN CEMETERY

" Harsh grief doth pass in time into far music "

DEAR, kindly eyes, that love has taught to weep;
Sweet, pensive lips, that know not of disdain,
Heart that can hold, sacred and deep,
           Life's joy, life's pain.

Azaleas bloom; your odorous heliotrope
Loads the cool air with aromatic freight.
It seems the blossoms sing of love, of hope—
           Too late, too late.

Pure love that lived shall last the worlds away,
There is no parting for the souls once met;
Soon shall hope gild with tender, ambient ray
           The passions of regret.

And years shall come, not wholly sad, nor sere,
And knowledge of the tattered silken skein
Of life and death shall make more dearly dear
      Love's joy, love's pain.

SIC PASSIM

FALSITY, Folly, and Vanity,
Fates that govern our world of shame;
   A trinity formed by humanity—
   Falsity, Folly, and Vanity.

All life plays at this empty game,
Dancing or praying, the song's the same,
   Echoing over vitality,
   Laughing at pale morality,
Masking alike the gallant and maim.

Sober Master and dainty Dame
Whisper, smile, and give them name—
   Tact and *Mirth* and *Sanity*.
They know it not, but their triple aim
Is Falsity, Folly, Vanity.

COLLABORATION EN L'AIR

TO F. T. D.

LIFE's hopes and sorrows we have known,
We've laughed the laugh, held back the groan—
                Like others, masking.
And yet to us Time's changing dial
Showed hours that grew cordial
                Without the asking.

Not when dear girls with kindly eyes
Join tears with laughter, smiles with sighs,
                Though that's delightful.
Nor yet when enemies lie low,
Unseated by our *jeux-de-mots*,
                We're not *too* spiteful.

But that sweet time, quite late at e'en,
Which comes to neither saint, I ween,
                Nor total sinner:
You know the hour, old chap, I think,
When thought to thought we quickly link—
                Well, after dinner.

43

When pipes of trusty cherry-wood
Do all they can to make us good
        And leave us purer—
Giving us aid o'er passes rocky,
Teaching us subtle ways to jockey
        Cold *atra cura*.

Snug by the fire, in slippered ease,
We've planned the sweets of life to seize—
        Those toys so brittle.
What if, out there, 'midst *sturm und drang*,
We've felt the pinch and known the pang,
        And failed—a little,

Within our world of smoky dreams
Are ways delicious, potent schemes,
        And lightsome laughter :
What clever plots we've limned, ah, me !
They *should* have echoed merrily
        Here—and hereafter.

But these have drifted with our smoke,
Ending, perchance, in some light joke
        Which we thought witty :

While in the air they made us gay,
Evanishing with dawn of day—
> A doubtful pity.

Well, well, come fill your pipe again,
Not heeding now the joy or pain
> Of loser, winner:
If in our day there still be time
For what is good—love, laughter, rhyme—
> 'Tis after dinner.

EILEEN'S EYES

My Eileen's eyes are laughing-bright,
Now all the world runs gaily dight.
> A word will make them softly grave;
> But tender-true and always brave
> Are Eileen's eyes.

* * * *

While merry's the mood, an engaging sprite
Will boldly grant me the boon I crave,
> Then leave me all in the sadder plight,
> Ah! . . . Eileen's eyes.

TO A LADY AT HER PIANO

ATHWART the keys of ivory
Your pink-tipped fingers seize
The very soul of melody
      Athwart the keys.

And we—who know of life's dark lees,
Of cold Fate's bitter irony,
Of hopes the world will ne'er appease,

You wake in us old memory
Of love we learned by dear degrees;
Ah! sweet's the little hand so free
      Athwart the keys.

TRIOLETS

DEAR Lou, do you remember,
When our total years were few,
How you loved some verses slender?
Dear Lou, do you remember
How you used to read and render
The tale, " If I were you "?
Ah, dear, do you remember
Time when our years were few?

When song could fill our hearts
With sense of pleasure true,—
Thwart life fell sunny darts,
When song could fill our hearts.
Time sped, birds piped in parts,
The summers came—and flew—
When song could fill our hearts
With sense of pleasure true.

47

I send the wit of many
With wishes good to you.
An you're pleased by all or any,
I send the wit of many.
May it prove good company
In its suit of Quaker hue.
I send the wit of many
With wishes good to you.

AN OLD-FASHIONED COMPLIMENT

WHITE roses and red I send
To garland a dainty head
That might some of its own grace lend
White roses and red.

MY DEAREST FLIRT

TO N. B.

My dearest Flirt hath shy brown een,
She's proud and petite, piquant and pert;
Her smile hints, "Ah! but it might have been."
     My dearest Flirt.

She knoweth of glances tender, keen;
Of the love that many would fain assert;
Of the play—before and behind the scene.

Yet she beareth her knowledge like Fairy Queen.
She is coy or careless, courteous or curt;
Her hand is for all, but her heart I've seen—
     My dearest Flirt.

ROPES OF SAND

*In answer to a picture of Amaryllis dancing and the
injunction to—*

> " Jog on, jog on, the footpath way,
>   And merrily hent the stile-a ;
> A merry heart goes all the day,
>   Your sad tires in a mile-a."—*Winter's Tale.*

DEAR May, another stile is hent, a year is over ;
We've striven and we've wrought ; we've left un-
    done ;
Anow we've buckled to, then laughingly turned
    rover
        And loitered in the sun.

To jogging manhood such poor fate is given :
We've loved and trusted, we have lost and won,
Dear ties that bound us lie asunder riven,
        Hopes—spat upon.

Maybe we've thought with Art's lithe pole to
    spring
Upon the stile of Fame—a tottering gateway;
But picture, verse, or prose lacks the true ring,
      And fails us straightway.

We've fallen back battered, battered but not hope-
    less,
A merry heart next obstacle shall carry;
While there be sands we cannot quite be ropeless,
      So weave—and tarry.

Jog, leap, or tumble, soon the last of stiles is hent,
Down into the earth six foot on t'other side;
Our hopes, desires, dreams, regrets, are spent—
      And scattered wide.

A New-Year wish is that I fain would send,
In place is scribbled down a silly wail;
And yet, I know the kindness of a friend
      Who'll never fail.

Dear thoughts and wishes fair to you, your heart
    a-merry,
Leap your life-stile as nature may suggest ;
Live bright as some sweet sparkling winter berry,
    Lips ripe . . . *for jest.*

TO A DELIGHTFULLY YOUNG LADY

LIL asked me to-day
To write her some verses.
Heigh-ho ! that's the way,
Lil asked *me* to-day.
In a year or two, say,
The question reverses,
Yet Lil asks me *to-day*
To write her some verses.

A MAN'S REASON.

TO V. H. G.

" *L'amour a passé par-là.*"

WHY do I wear this coat? you say.
I always shall. I know I swore it
Oft, in the studio that day
   When Viola wore it.

It's making somewhat t'ward decay,
And every Spring the winds are colder—
I'm warmed by thinking: " Once it lay
   Athwart *her* shoulder."

The velvet of the collar's old,
Yet, still with all its faults, I love it.
Once little hairy rings of gold
   Peer'd coy above it.

Ah, round about the sleeves enough
Of light o' love still lingers,
For out beneath this coarse old cuff
   Peeped·rose-tipp'd fingers.

53

You hint the thing is quite antique—
Not cut to match with modish taste ;
I'll answer " that " for fashion's freak—
  It zoned *her* waist.

And so I wear it, sans remorse ;
I'll use no other overcoat,
For *this* was fastened close across
  Dear Viola's throat.

Envoi

But if, perchance, you'd care to know
A fact I thought romance might smother,
Lend me thine ear, in whisper low—
  I have no other.

A SOLENT SONG

REMINISCENT OF DAMP FIREWORKS AND
COMPENSATIONS

*A big steam yacht, moored near the West Cowes Roads.
The characters—a Redfern-made girl, with Irish eyes,
and a man in ordinary yachting dress; they are
standing on the stairs of the bridge; he is protecting
her from wind and rain. The evening is grey and
wet. The yachts and other vessels in distance are
half illuminated with Bengal lights; rockets and
other fireworks are seen intermittently. Behind is
East Cowes, with vague suggestion of Osborne Towers
and wooded park.*

To shore, to sea, afar the fireworks flare,
Half seen in transit through the rainy air:
But your sweet eyes make sweet the gloomy scene,
Eileen.

The harbour's dull with smoke; 'neath clouded sky,
Athwart the sea grey sweeping gulls go by:
Tell me, I pray, what may those bright eyes mean,
Eileen?

I care not for the blustering wind
Or drifting rain, so that those kind
Eyes hint a joy all unforeseen,
                    Eileen.

They tell, I think, how they the lattice are
Of a sweet soul within more clear by far,
Or, maybe, they a fickle heart do screen,
                    Eileen.

Perchance, some day they'll worlds of love unclose,
Perchance their tenderness is just a pose:
Yet on their trustful truth I'm fain to lean,
                    Eileen.

How can I doubt the Irish blue
Of eyes whose softness bids me sue—
Eyes that have beckon'd mine, I ween,
                    Eileen.

Ah ! would it were my art to truly trace
A shining soul 'neath your dear piquant face,
Plumbing the starry depths with glance so keen,
                    Eileen.

That I for once—for once and all—could tell
Whether or no they merely were a . . . " sell."
If you're coquette, then I despair of e'en
Eileen.

Envoi

Heigh-ho ! a while Love crowned the prow,
We'll own that " Paradise enow."
We go our ways : it " might-have-been,"
Eileen.

TO MANY EYES

To many eyes I've sung a lay,
To many girls in merry guise :
Welcome I've given—well-a-day !—
    To many eyes.

Let those who can, the vain despise,
Let those who will, refuse to pay
Tribute of laughter and of sighs.

Life's sterner joys we cast away,
I'll own we are not overwise ;
Yet I'll deny, an you should say,
    " Too many eyes."

SHADOWS

A Recitation with Dances written for Miss Florence Bourne

CHRISTMAS OF THE PRESENT YEAR

Before the curtain is drawn up, the music of the very latest thing in rapid waltzes is heard. The scene is a stately ballroom in an old castle. As the servants extinguish the candles, the moonlight floods through the tall windows and lies in pools of opaline colour upon the polished black oak floor and faintly illuminates the musicians' gallery at the end of the salon. From the mysterious shadows of the gallery, a delicate figure, clad in a dainty dress of the middle of last century, is seen to glide down the stairway and across the ballroom. She looks about her, recognising the scene of many conquests past, and merry days that have flown. She trips along through the moonlight, she flirts her fan, shrugs a pretty shoulder, and makes a little moue.

AT last the dancers of to-day
Have tired of our dear old hall.
How sweet the silence, sweet the way
The moonlight and the shadows fall!

The music of a minuet is heard.

59

On such a glistening floor 'tis bliss
To dance like this, to dance like this.

Dances.

How oddly rang their tunes to-night,
They trip and turn a deal too fast;
I wonder can they find delight
In whirling till all breath is past.

Gone's the *bel air* of my fresh youth,
Now men grow hot, and red, and rude,
The girls are pretty—but, in truth,
I vow their steps are all too crude.

Music of some old measure is heard.

She has not learned, the modern miss,
To dance like this, to dance like this.

Dances.

So long ago, those olden days,
When I was really flesh and blood,
Methinks I have forgot some ways
Of happiness, that made life good.

Well I recall a distant time
When gladness lived in heart and brain;
Through Life's dance flowed so sweet a rhyme,
I fain would haunt old earth again.

So here I glide when light is spent;
They guess not of my passing near,—
Tho' lovers tell of subtle scent
From a rose of yester-year.

Oft have I wished in summer days
To mingle with this later race,
Who see my portrait there, and praise
The beauty of the Lady Grace.

They know me not; tho' at midnight hour
I've heard them talk of another ghost.
'Tis grim Sir Raymond; in the tower
He slew his kinsman and his host.

An ancestor, sure, but years before
I came to the Castle he'd passed away:
I only bow when we meet. There's gore
On the track of his steps, they say.

The air of a lively country dance is heard.

He is too wicked and old, I wis,
To dance with me, to dance like this.

Dances.

So I foot my measure, *à solitaire;*
Tho' there's one I know who'd like to come.
The reason he fought, was a lock of hair,
That matched my own, said some.

I loved him not in the days agone:
That night he died . . . 'Twas here he stood.
In the morn the brow I had joked upon
Was stained with his own life's blood.

Oh yes, I grieved, in thoughtless fashion;
To jest, to dance, was my desire.
Poor boy, I laughed at his fervid passion,
I laughed, and bade the world admire.

Old Time, you ring the changes still;
Sure, could he come this very night
His heavy heart I'd try to fill
With joy, and set our lives aright.

Hist ! 'tis his form beside the door,—
He comes at last.   Once more we've met.
Dear Hugh, life's gone.   Let's take the floor
And dance, tho' late, our minuet.

> *The music of the minuet is heard more*
> *softly than at first.*

Ghosts have forgotten how to kiss,
But we can dance : yes, dance like this.

> *They dance.*

CURTAIN.

LOVE AND DEATH

The Picture by F. G. Watts, R.A.

O LOVE and Death,
Calm with uplifted hand, the mother, angel, friend,
Advances t'wards Life's portals.   See her bend
O'er the young Love, who'd fain the house defend.

Impotent Love cries burning tears of rage,
But conquering Death, the kindly, certain, sage,
Bids Love regard her as his appanage.

Love learns not, but with tender strength opposes
The passing of the Stranger o'er the roses ;
Still Death moves on, and as she wills, disposes.

O Love and Death,
Be reconciled, each guarding well the other.
O Love and Death, strong sister, tenderest brother.

LONDON MAIDS

I.—THE "A B C" MAID

SHE's pale and neat; she's dressed in black :
  She comes to your table wearily,
With pensive air, but a modern knack
  Of hinting all life's vacuity.

      She carries no old-world courtesy,
      But the air is freighted odorously,
      For they give one excellent tea
      In the sober *salons* of "A B C."

In convent garb of black and white
  By the counter, where urns work steamily,
She waits and watches—morn till night—
  She's quick, yet her eyes move dreamily.

      She gives no heed to a pleasantry,
      She returns a guest's gratuity,—
      But she brings one excellent tea
      In the sober *salons* of "A B C."

She'll hardly answer ; her smile soon fades.
  She foregoes all mundane vanity.
Ah ! subtle sphinx among London maids,
  Who shall guess what your riddle be ?

      'Neath that stoic calm does the heart beat
          free ?
      Could you tell us of hope—or of agony ?
      Could you tell how they make it, the
          excellent tea,
      In the sober *salons* of " A B C " ?

II.—THE VISITING GOVERNESS

Early she journeys from Camden Town,
  Brisk and pretty, supple and slim.
She's busy *en route* with the missing noun ;
  She'll glance at the " *dictée* "—a " theme " she'll skim,
Casting a look at the lesson-book,
  Or loosing her thoughts on a casual whim.

The carmen have learnt her morning hour ;
  They guard the corner she always fills.
Fine days or wet days have no power
  To alter her ways—the ways she wills.
She travels afar in her rumbling car,
  T'wards Grosvenor Gate from the Camden Hills.

Confident, clever, and cool is she,
  And learned in much of the Girton lore,
A Grad of the newest school is she—
  Yet bears no taint of the 'Varsity bore :
The *savoir-faire* of her graceful air
  Tells one as much—and hints far more.

As she passes on with a courage sweet,
 'Mid a world of chance, thro' a web of Fate—
Ah, how she brightens Life's gloomiest street!
 For a maid more merry, yet sane, sedate,
You may look for long in the crowding throng
 Of Camden Town—or of Grosvenor Gate!

III.—THE TYPEWRITER

The window shows a legal street
  Where children run from the beadle's cane :
Where hansoms wait, where lawyers meet,
  Chatter their gossip, and part again.

A hundred faces pass by outside ;
  But quite unconscious of all of these,
The untiring typist's trade is plied
  With dancing hands on the letter'd keys.

The words fly forth with a click, click, click ;
  The whirr of the " carriage " the air is filling,
While the restless bell and the fingers' trick
  Make an impression " frightfully thrilling."

IV.—FLOWER-GIRLS.

Flower-girls call in the street,
Where the East and the West End meet;
The policeman goes by on his beat,
They move to a distance discreet.
" Violets, sweet!   Violets, sweet! "
Flower-girls call in the street.

They stand where the traffic increasing flows ;
With the pomp of bedraggled plumes they're clad ;
They light up the road till it gorgeously glows,
With mimosa and jonquille and delicate rose—
　　　　To make other people glad.

Flower-girls call in the street,
(Weary voices, and wet, worn feet,)
" Penny a button-hole, all complete! "
Flower-girls call in the street.

If they be coarse and vulgar, fond of row ;
If their strident air all fancy slaughters ;—

Of spring-time glories they carry enow
To shelter their failings, and e'en to endow
                    With beauty—beauty's daughters.

    Flower-girls call in the street,
    They bully, and wrangle, and cheat ;
    Flower-girls call in the street—
    The blossoms whose odour is fleet.
    Men laugh as they pass, and repeat :—
    " All purity fades in the street."

V.—THE PROGRAMME MAID.

When the theatre's lighted, the gilding a-glare,
She comes to your aid with a grace *débonnaire* :
She points you the way to a plush-cover'd chair,
　　　　　　And she offers you glasses.
Though her costume is quiet, of black or of brown,
It's a " note " in the scene—and yon gay, garish
　　gown
(Intended to ring in the ears of the town)
　　　　　　Ineffectively passes.

As the fiddles are busy with light overture,—
She hunts for the number, your stall to secure—
You note that her apron is wrought in guipure,
　　　　　　That her manner is polished ;
Her cap does not tell of a drear servitude,
It's exceedingly *chic*. She will hardly intrude—
But I *think* she can hint of a sweet gratitude,
　　　　　　Though all fees are abolished.

She is rapid and bright; *chastement corsettée*,
An you try, you will find she has plenty to say
As she gives you a smile and a bill of the play.
                    And she knows, quite by heart,
The Comedy *musicale* now on the stage,
And sneers at the lady who's playing the page :
She's younger, more pretty, and could, I'll engage,
                    Fill as lively a part.

VI.—THE POST OFFICE CLERK.

Behind your grille of lattice work
  You ply your trade with hearty will;
Anon you frown, anon you smirk,
            Behind your grille.

Like prison'd bird you pause and trill,
  When leisure comes; you preen and perk,
Adjust a lock or smooth a frill.

An commerce pours, you do not shirk;
  Then runs the ever ready quill;
Sure, much of happiness may lurk
            Behind your grille.

VII.—THE NURSEMAID

To the outer world she comes in view
 When chestnuts bloom, when birds are trilling,
When nature is seen in its gayest hue,
                    And the Parks are filling.

In a merry meeting she takes her place;
 Dear little sons and dear little daughters—
Laughing, tumbling—sparkle and race
                    Like the fountain's waters.

When the sun shines bright through the delicate
        green,
 When the sunshade's white against blue,
I' the cool of the morning are sure to be seen
                    These ambulant two.

She tenderly watches her charge a-crow,
 Untouched by cynic modernity;
Each kindly gesture goes to show
                    The instinct of maternity.

Her gifts are more sterling than outward charm ;
  On baby she pours her devotion,
Noting, all day, with gentle alarm,
          His slightest emotion.

Sturdily, bravely, she goes her ways,
  Generous, kindly, of even pace ;
And the gorgeous drama in which she plays
          Is " The Coming Race."

VIII.—READING MAID AT BRITISH MUSEUM

Beneath the dome Panizzi planned,
   Each day she makes her busy home—
With all the largest books to hand
         Beneath the dome.

Perchance she longs afield to roam,
   Out on the shore to take her stand,
And watch the surf lash up in foam.

But she has joined our writing band,
   And follows Fame (that tricksy gnome
Who haunts the air—capricious, bland)
         Beneath the dome.

BLACK AND TAN

For a picture by Mr. Ludovici, showing a girl with black and tan terrier in her arms.

JACK, soliloquising :

How is't, I wonder, all our pleasures fade ?
I'm very small, but every inch a terrier,—
Yet here I'm held in fairest *gants de Suède*.
Oh ! for a rougher life—oh ! for a merrier.

I used to own a master up at Cam,
And often had a day with rat or rabbit.
He sent me to *her ;* and so here I am
Growing a lap-dog by the very habit.

But we small *canes* know a thing or two.
Ah ! when he comes a-courting here next Vac.
I shall be free to do as I would do ;
I shall withdraw to please the other Jack.

Heigho ! these humans seem a droll division ;
My master loves the lass, and she adores me.
I'd like to whisper him my own decision,
That she is very sweet, but sadly bores me.

"The wood gods watched how joy dragged
How bitter the uneven duel."

A WOODMAN LOVED

Ballade from the unacted tragedy " Reaping "

A WOODMAN loved a lady fair
Of wanton mood. This wayward maid
Could guile him on to mad despair—
Many a light love-freak she played.
" Ah, Life," he cried, "your pleasures fade.
What worth the crown without its jewel ? "
He cursed the Fates in woody glade—
" Sure sprites be kind, as well as cruel ? "

The wood gods answered from their lair :
" We grant you her for whom you prayed.
Mate for a while and go a-pair—
Until we come to be repaid."
" Ye gods," he cried, " all, all is laid
Before your shrines ; my soul is fuel
To feed your fires. Who is't has said
Sprites are not kind as well as cruel ? "

Lust hurried out with scorching flare,
With lambent flame, with flashing raid,
Until all joys evanished ; there
A silvern pall, white ashes stayed.
The woman's sweets lay disarrayed,
Her heart showed black as any tewel—
" I've pawned a soul in wrongful trade.
Sprites are not kind—but they are cruel."

Envoi

The wood gods watched how joy decayed,
How bitter the uneven duel.
They laughed : " We take the wanton jade,
Give back your soul,—sprites are not cruel."

LOVE SAILS AWAY

A song, set to music by Miss Conroy

Down, down by the shore where the breakers beat
 In musical rhyme o'erflowing,
We bade each adieu, our hearts beat true
 To an air of Love's own knowing;
 Adieu, adieu, to my sailor true,
With tears at heart, but a smile for you.
 Adieu, adieu, for a sailor's true,
  On land or on sea,
  Ah me, ah me!

Away to the West with its silvern sheen
 My dear heart's-love is flying,
As I kiss my hand, where the golden band
 Of our plighted troth is lying;
 Away, away, for many a day,
Till Winter's chang'd to Spring-time's May.
 Adieu, adieu, is a sailor true?
  On land or on sea,
  Ah me, ah me!

'Mid April's changes, 'neath August's glow,
    Full long I watched by the murm'ring sea ;
But a lover flown is a rose o'erblown,
    Alas and alas, that this must be !
Love sailed away, for that vessel gay
Held a heart for me that has gone for aye.
    Adieu, adieu, to my sailor true,
        On land or on sea
        No more to me.
    To my heart, adieu ! Ah ! a sailor is true
    Until he has sailed across the sea.

TO RED WINE IN A SILVER BOWL

A topaz draught in a silvern cup—
(Hot life zoned by a pallid pale) :
Ah, Time ironic will have his sup,
A topaz draught from a silvern cup.
But while all nature fills it up,
None turn glance to the threatening flail,
From a topaz draught in silvern cup—
Hot life zoned by a pallid pale.

WE TWO

"There be good fellows in the world, an a man could
light on them."

WE were a pair of friends: ah me!
Friends who would never sever.
We linked our arms continually;
I talked, Jack listened, frequently.
We did not always quite agree,
'Twas not my fault, however.

I often told my hopes to Jack:
How Fame and Fortune I would win,
How I the world of fools would rack,
How in the years to come no lack
Of honours should fill up the sack
Of his friend Benjamin.

He'd smoke, and sneer, and smile,
Assume an air of squalor,
Let me talk on for half-a-mile,

G 2

Then hold out what he named his "tile,"
And hint that of this future pile
He'd now beg—half-a-dollar.

Whene'er I told of coming book—
Wherein my wisdom lashed at folly—
He'd curl himself in cosy nook
And give me just a sleepy look,
And say that "Wisdom he'd forsook,
Because the fools were jolly."

I'd stir him with dramatic thought,
I'd tell him of romances,
Of whimsies that my brain had caught,
Of battles that my wits had fought,
Of lessons that the sages taught,
Of sly or lurid fancies.

I sang him songs of Arcadie,—
My Arcadie, a land afar—
Where man and maid roamed fancy free
Where pipe and lute made music : he
Broke in—" Now, Ben, I'll trouble ye,
My pipe is out, for a cigar."

Once as 'midst hills we toured about,
I paused to point *the* view in Wales,
I know I felt inclined to spout,
The picturesque he should *not* flout.
He gently took his penknife out
And neatly pared his nails !

Later, when Love his silken bond
Entangled with my heart strings,
I told old Jack of my dear blonde,
How sweet she was, how over-fond,
How our two souls did aye respond,—
He murmured, " Ah, Love *has* wings."

One day I sought Madge at her cot—
Oft from our tryst she tarried—
I sang, " My Lady of Shalott,
Hie to the arms of Lancelot."
She smiled, " Dear Ben, I'd *rather* not,
For Jack and I have married."

I laid my hand upon my breast
To save my heart from breaking ;

I bid the twain be doubly blest—
But to myself I then confessed
I'd give their love a shaking.

I vowed I'd soon revengèd be:
Last night I bade old Jack to tea,
I plied old Jack with rare whiskey,
I lured him on to *eau de vie*,
I told him many a wild storee.

My whilom friend grows queer, alack!
My whilom friend in cab I pack,—
I pack him in, I steal his key,
I send him home to Margarie
What time the clocks are striking three.

Envoi

I know the dear girl perfectly.
Ha, ha, I am revenged. But he?
                    Poor Jack—poor Jack!

VILLANELLES OF VANITY

I.—SOMEBODY KNOWS

A pretty girl before her glass is about to add a touch of
rouge to an already satisfactory complexion.

To blanch the lily, to rouge the rose,
To brighten Nature with subtle Art,—
Such are the vanities Somebody knows.

Somebody perched in a delicate pose,
Armed with a hare's-foot, ready to start
To blanch the lily, to rouge the rose.

To add a little to lovers' woes,
To polish the tip of Dan Cupid's dart :
Such are the vanities Somebody knows.

To see that her beauty gracefully flows
To an exquisite centre—hers the part
To blanch the lily, to rouge the rose.

The haunting touch of the feet of crows,
The tiny blemish that *won't* depart :
Such are the vanities Somebody knows.

Heigh-ho! the *toilette* has tender throes,
But they pass as one turns with a merry heart
To blanch the lily, to rouge the rose :
Such are the vanities Somebody knows.

II.—WHICH OF THE TWO?

*A lady before the fire in her dressing-room: the maid waits
while she makes her choice between two evening gowns—
one cut high, the other cut low.*

Which of the two, the staid or the gay?
Either will capture a dozen beaux.
Should it be chaste or *décolletée* ?

For an elderly Crœsus, growing grey,
For a youthful guardsman who loves, I trow,—
Which of the two, the staid or the gay?

There are poets who sing, and parsons who pray;
I care not for sermons, nor sweet rondeau.
Should it be chaste or *décolletée* ?

There are those whose raptures I'd fain delay;
There are those who often become *de trop*.
Which of the two, the staid or the gay?

If only *he* would his will betray—
The lord of my heart. Ah! then I would know
Should it be chaste or *décolletée*.

From over the sea he returns to-day ;
And his present taste ?   (How one's troubles grow !)
Which of the two, the staid or the gay ?
Should it be chaste or *décolletée ?*

III.—THE WAY TO WOO

O maiden of the dainty shoe,
And hosen of carnation clocks,
Teach us the potent way to woo.

Should man advance with cap askew,
With air bizarre or orthodox,
O maiden of the dainty shoe?

Will best of luck to him accrue
Who prates aloud of " shares " and " stocks " ?
Teach us the potent way to woo.

Dost love the pose of " dare and do,"
Or psychologic paradox,
O maiden of the dainty shoe?

Would it be wise to send—*à vous*—
A ruby bangle, bonnets, frocks?
Teach us the potent way to woo.

But I incline to boldly sue
The right to guard you from Life's shocks.
O maiden of the dainty shoe,
You teach the potent way to woo!

TO A COUNTRY MUSE

WHERE runs the brook athwart the wood
With silver secret for each nook—
I near forgot my worldlihood
        Where runs the brook.

There, when the fresh young hazels shook
With song the thrushes poured in flood:
In your clear eyes I stayed to look . . . .

They told me all you could and would,
An I the townward path forsook.
I was the fool who turned : you stood
        Where runs the brook.

ADIEU

To Richard Matthew Dudley Fell

" . . . . till my last of lines is penn'd,
 . . . . love, grief, laughter, at an end,
Whene'er I write your name, may I write friend."

WE'VE laughed away the old men's saws,
We've grinned at young men's poses;
We've mocked at the Mosaic laws
And pagan " Love and Roses."

We've laughed at men who've won their way,
At failing men, at stoics;
We've jeered the puny roundelay,
Guffawed at the Heroics.

We've laughed at foes—at friends as well,
At Wisdom's shafts, at Folly's elves:
We've laughed at Heaven and at hell—
But loudest laughed at our own selves.

For Fortune's poor essays to aid,
For biting disappointment,
For general bitterness, we've said—
Laughter's the only ointment.

And so we've laughed wi' tongue i' the cheek,
At all our hopes and all our fears :
The reason is not far to seek,
Since laughter masks the rising tears.

*   *   *

So ran the London life we mourn,
Compact of weary striving,
But "out there" you shall find the bourne
Ample and peaceful—thriving.

And then across New Zealand's plain—
Across the plains primeval—
Shall laugh, maybe, in happier vein,
Kick sadness to the devil.

*   *   *

Adieu, dear friend of many days,
Of mine own mood, but truer,
May fresh-born Fortune light your ways
In broader lands and newer.

May life assume its rightful guise,
Unwarped by cynic neighbour;
Ah, may we grow uncommon wise
And earn delight—of labour.

À VOUS

Dear Chloë of the wavy hair,
That painters paint, that poets sing :
Dear Chloë, blithe and debonair,
To thee I wing
My fragile story, writ with care,
My little book, alas ! for gift to thee,
A paltry thing.
Others may hymn thy shining eyes,
All-conquering smile,
Thy constant beauty and surprise :
And judge they gain the greatest prize
With metric guile.
'Tis not their skill that I despise,
Not skill, nor style.
But merely this, that all their song
Is song external.
They know not what fair views belong
To the eternal
Chambers within thy heart, where throng
Sweets that could make hell heavenliwise,
An thou wert by, dense night diurnal,
An thou wert gone, fair lawns of Paradise
Infernal.